This book belongs to

....

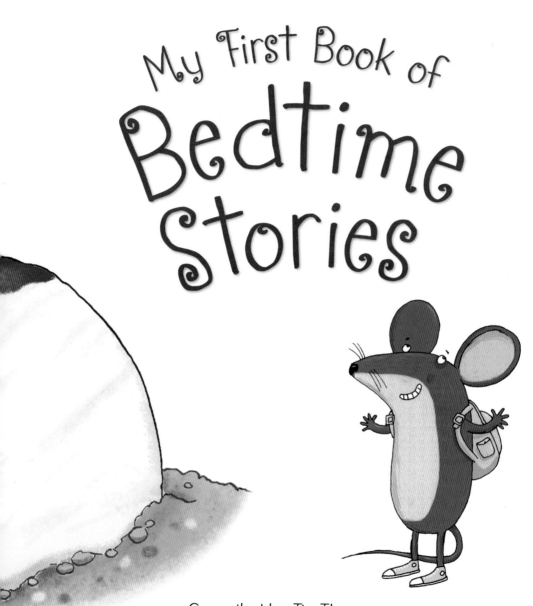

My First Book of Bedtime Stories

Compiled by Tig Thomas

Miles Kelly

First published in 2017 by Miles Kelly Publishing Ltd
Harding's Barn, Bardfield End Green, Thaxted, Essex, CM6 3PX, UK

This edition printed 2018

2 4 6 8 10 9 7 5 3

Publishing Director Belinda Gallagher
Creative Director Jo Cowan
Editorial Director Rosie Neave
Senior Editor Sarah Parkin
Design Manager Joe Jones
Production Elizabeth Collins, Caroline Kelly
Reprographics Stephan Davis, Jennifer Cozens, Thom Allaway
Assets Lorraine King

ISBN 978-1-78617-319-5

Printed in China

British Library Cataloguing-in-Publication Data
A catalogue record for this book is available from the British Library

Made with paper from a sustainable forest

www.mileskelly.net

CONTENTS

Once Upon a Time

Strange and Silly

Animal Antics

Tricks and Teases

Once Upon a Time

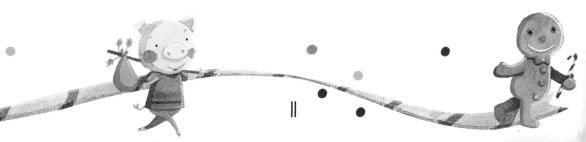

Sleeping Beauty

Once upon a time, a king and queen had a beautiful baby girl. They loved her very much.

The king and queen invited the twelve fairies in the kingdom to the baby's christening. But

they didn't invite the thirteenth fairy, who was mean.

On the day of the christening, every fairy came to give the princess a special gift. One wished that she would always be happy, another wished that she would be loved all her life. One by one they gave the princess their wishes.

They had nearly finished when the door burst open and the

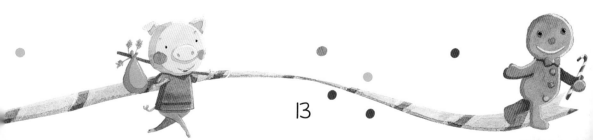

mean fairy walked in. She was very cross at being missed out of the party.

The bad fairy walked up to the baby's cradle and said, "Let me give her a gift too. I say that when the princess is fifteen, she will prick her finger on a spindle and fall down dead." Then

she walked out.
Everyone was
very upset! But
the twelfth fairy
came forward.

"I have not yet given my
gift," she said. "I cannot take
away the bad wish, but I can
change it a little. The princess
will not die. Instead she will sleep
for a hundred years until she is
woken by a true love's kiss."

"But if she doesn't wake for a hundred years, no one will be there when she wakes up and our castle will be in ruins," said the queen.

"I will arrange it so that everyone goes to sleep with her, and that the castle and everything in it are there when she wakes up," said the fairy.

The king was so worried about the bad fairy's wish that he

arranged for all spindles in the kingdom to be burned.

The princess grew up and everyone loved her. She laughed and sang all day long, and she was a kind and lovely young girl.

One day, when the princess was fifteen, she found a staircase in the castle that she had never seen before. She went up the stairs and found a little bedroom, and there she saw an old lady spinning wool onto a spindle. Of course, it was the mean fairy in disguise.

"What's this funny thing?" the princess asked, and she touched the spindle. At that moment, she pricked her finger on it and fell onto the bed, fast asleep.

At the same time, everyone in the castle fell asleep – the king on his throne, the queen with her ladies in waiting, the

cook in the kitchen, and the horses in the stable.

At the same time, a thick hedge of thorny bushes grew up around the castle. It was completely hidden, and after a few years, all the people of the land forgot it was there.

One day one hundred years later, a prince came riding by. He saw the hedge and decided to chop his way through with his sword. The thorns ripped at his clothes, but he kept going.

Finally, the prince was through the hedge. He walked into the palace, which was now covered in dust and cobwebs. Everywhere, people were sleeping. Even the birds in the garden and the flies on the windowsills were asleep.

The prince eventually came to a little bedroom in a tower.

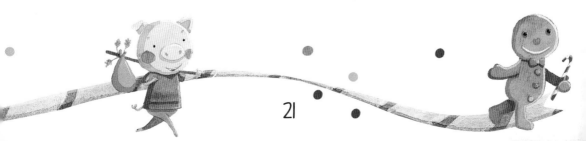

On the bed in this room was the most beautiful girl he had ever seen, lying asleep. In that moment, he fell in love with her.

The prince bent down and kissed the princess. As soon as he did this, she opened her eyes, and in that moment, she fell in love with him.

They walked down through the palace together, where everyone had woken up now.

When they found the king and queen, the prince asked permission to marry their daughter. The king and queen happily agreed.

The wedding took place one week later, and they invited all the fairies to the celebrations - except the bad one.

The Gingerbread Man

Once upon a time a woman was doing some baking. She took a big piece of delicious, gingery dough, rolled it out, and shaped it into a little man. Then she stuck in two brown currants

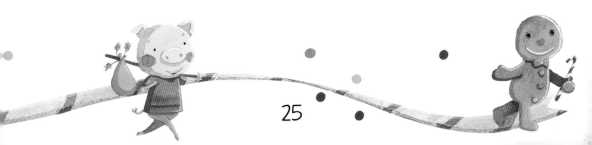

for his eyes, and decorated his face and body.

But just as the woman was about to put him into the oven, he jumped down from the baking tray and ran away, saying, "Run, run, as fast as you can. You can't catch me, I'm the gingerbread man."

"Stop him!" shouted the woman to her husband.

The man made a grab for the gingerbread man, but he ran on, saying, "Run, run as fast as you can. You can't catch me, I'm the gingerbread man. I've run faster than a woman and I can run faster than you." And he ran on laughing.

The man couldn't catch the gingerbread man, but he

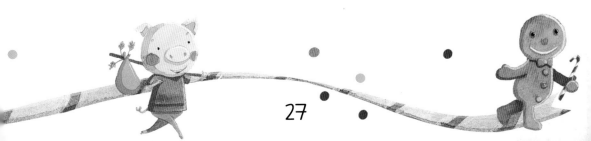

shouted to his children, who
were playing in the garden,
"Stop that gingerbread man!"
The children ran after him,
but he said, "Run, run, as fast as
you can. You can't catch me, I'm
the gingerbread

man. I've run faster than a woman and a man, and I can run faster than you." And he ran on, laughing.

The children couldn't catch the gingerbread man, but they saw their dog by the gate, so they shouted, "Dog! Stop that gingerbread man!"

So the dog ran after the

gingerbread man, but he said, "Run, run, as fast as you can. You can't catch me, I'm the gingerbread man. I've run faster than a woman and a man and the children, and I can run faster than you." And he ran on, laughing.

As the gingerbread man ran along, he came to a river. "I can't cross that!" he said. "If I get wet, I'll crumble away to nothing." So he stopped running.

Just then a clever old fox came up. "I'll give you a lift across the river," he said. "Climb onto my back and I'll swim you across." So the gingerbread man climbed onto the fox's back.

Halfway across the river, the fox said, "Gingerbread man, I'm swimming low in the water. Climb up onto my neck and you won't get wet." So the gingerbread man climbed onto the fox's neck.

Now the fox started to smell the delicious smell of the gingerbread man, and he felt very hungry.

When they were three quarters of the way across, he said, "The water is getting deeper. Climb round onto my forehead." And the gingerbread man climbed onto the fox's forehead. He was very near the fox's mouth now.

As they got near to the other side of the river, the fox said, "Just climb down onto my nose. Then I know you'll be safe." So the gingerbread man climbed right down to the fox's nose.

And then the fox threw his head up, so the gingerbread

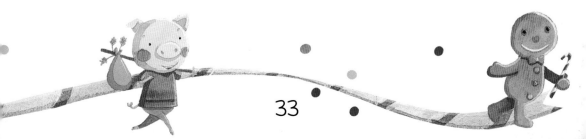

man flew up in the air, and the
fox opened his mouth, ready to
gobble the gingerbread man
down. But then
the gingerbread

man gave a little wriggle in the air, and landed on the bank on the other side of the river.

He danced and he twirled and then he ran away, laughing and saying, "Run, run, as fast as you can. You can't catch me, I'm the gingerbread man."

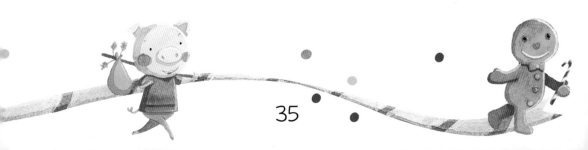

The Crow

Once upon a time there were three princesses. They were all young and beautiful, but the youngest was the kindest.

A little way from the palace in which they lived there was a castle. It was old and broken down, and no one lived in it. But the garden was full of beautiful flowers, and the youngest princess often went to walk there.

One day, when she was looking at the flowers, a black crow hopped out of a rose bush in front of her. The poor bird's wings were torn and bleeding, and the kind little princess was sad for it.

When the crow saw this it turned to her and said, "I am not really a black crow, but a prince, who has been turned into a crow by a witch. If you were willing, Princess, you could save me. But you would have to say goodbye to your family and come and live in this ruined castle. There is one room in it that's fit to live in, in which there is a golden bed. You would have to stay there all by yourself, and no matter what you see, you must never cry out or scream or make any noise."

The kind princess agreed, and after returning home to say goodbye to her family, she hurried back to the castle, and moved into the room with the golden bed.

When night came she lay down in the golden bed. At midnight the door opened and a fierce tiger entered the room,

growling and snarling at her. The princess lay quite still in the middle of the bed and did not say a word.

Then the tiger disappeared and a huge green snake came slithering straight towards her. The princess was frightened, but she never made a sound.

Next, there was a huge monster prowling round the room. Again, she kept quite still,

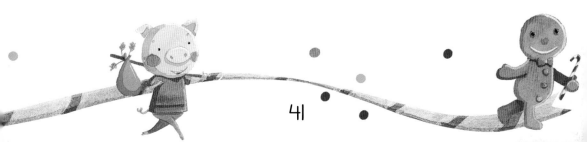

and soon this vanished too.

The next moment the crow appeared and hopped all round the room with joy. It thanked the princess, and said that the spell would be broken soon if she went on like this.

For several more nights, scary things appeared round the princess's bed, but she never said a word. After a few days one of the princess's older sisters came to visit her. The older princess decided to stay the night, but when the scary sights appeared, she screamed in terror, and the youngest princess nearly joined in. After that, she always kept watch alone. She might have been very lonely, but the crow visited her every day and talked to her.

One day the princess was in the garden, picking some flowers

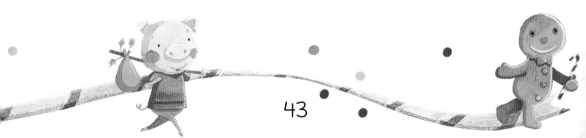

for her room, when a pale but
handsome young man came up
to her. He knelt down at her feet
and kissed her hands.

"I am the prince," he said,
"and you have saved me. I have
fallen in love with you over the
months you have helped me.
Will you marry me and come
and live with me in my castle?"

The princess happily agreed.
And as they turned around to

look at the castle, they saw it was no longer broken and old, but grand and

shining and new.

And there they lived for many years of joy and happiness.

Little Red Riding Hood

Once upon a time there was a little girl who always wore a riding cloak with a red hood, so everyone called her Little Red Riding Hood.

One day her mother said to

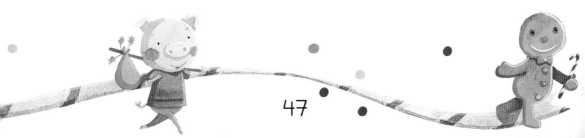

her, "Please go and visit your grandmother and take her this basket of food, because I hear she has been ill."

So Little Red Riding Hood put on her cloak and set off to walk through the woods to Grandma's house.

On the way, she met a wolf. The wolf was hungry, but he didn't dare eat Little Red Riding Hood because there were some woodcutters working nearby. So he asked her where she was going.

Little Red Riding Hood was scared, but she answered, "I am going to my grandmother's house on the other side of the wood." Then she ran quickly on her way.

The wolf ran as well, much quicker than Little Red Riding Hood, and he got to the house first. He locked grandmother in another room. Then he put on one of her spare nightdresses, her cap and her glasses, and got into her bed.

When Little Red Riding Hood

knocked at the cottage door,
the wolf was waiting.

"Come in, come in!" he said, in
a squeaky voice. "Is that my
Little Red Riding Hood? Come
closer, child."

Little Red Riding Hood took a
step closer. "Grandma! What big
arms you have!" she said.

"All the better to hug you
with, my dear," said the wolf.

Little Red Riding Hood took

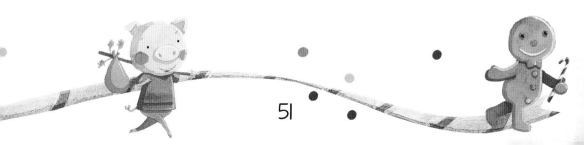

another step towards the bed. "And Grandma, what big ears you have."

"All the better to hear you with, my dear," said the wolf.

Little Red Riding Hood took another step towards the bed. "And Grandma, what big eyes you have."

"All the better to see you with, my dear," said the wolf.

"And Grandma, what big

teeth you have," said Little Red Riding Hood, going up close to the bed.

"All the better to *eat* you with," roared the wolf, jumping out of bed, ready to gobble down Little Red Riding Hood.

But just then the door burst open. In came a woodcutter with a big, sharp axe, and at once the wolf turned tail and ran away as fast as he could.

The woodcutter and Little Red Riding Hood found her real grandmother safe and sound. Then they all sat down to some tea, and that bad wolf was never seen again.

Rumpelstiltskin

One day a miller told a lie about his daughter, to make her seem more important.

"My daughter knows how to spin straw into gold!" the silly man boasted.

The king heard about this and he wanted to see it for himself, so he asked the girl to come to the palace.

When she got there, he showed her to a room piled with straw. He said, "Spin this into gold by tomorrow." Then he locked her in the room.

The girl started to cry, but then a funny little man appeared. He said he would help

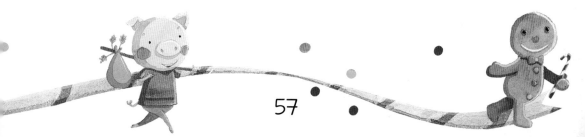

her if she gave
him her first-born
child. The miller's
daughter was so
frightened that she
agreed.

So the little man
sat down and spun
bundle after bundle
of straw into gold.

In the morning,
the king could

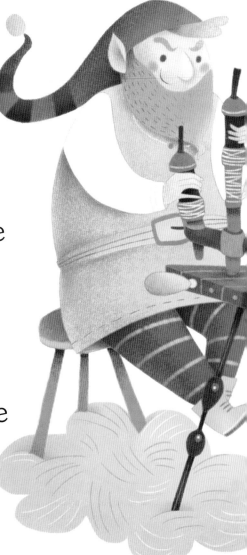

not believe his eyes. And the
next day he married the
miller's daughter.

After about a year, the
new queen gave birth to
a son and was very happy
- until the funny little man
suddenly appeared.

"Now you must give me
what you promised," he said.
The queen offered to give
him all kinds of treasure

instead of her son, but he refused it all.

In the end, she cried so much the little man said that if she could guess his name he would let her off. He would give her three guesses, and come back in three days to hear them.

All night, the queen thought about every name she had ever heard. She sent out messengers to search for the little man. But they all came back with no news.

Late on the last evening a messenger returned, and said to the queen, "I saw a little man singing in the woods. He sang, 'No one can guess that Rumpelstiltskin is my name!'"

"Saved!" said the queen, and she gave the messenger a big bag of gold.

When the little man appeared, she decided to tease

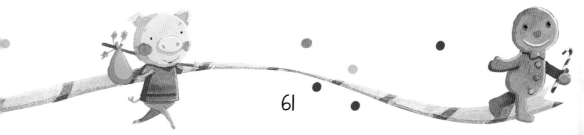

him. So she said, "Is your name Ebenezer?"

"No!" said the little man. "Give me your son."

"Is your name Methuselah?"

"No!" said the little man. "Give me your son."

The queen smiled. "Is there any chance that you could be called Rumpelstiltskin?"

"*Who told you?*" roared the little man. He jumped up and

down so hard that the ground beneath his feet split open and swallowed him up - and he was never seen again.

Chicken Licken

One fine day Chicken Licken went for a walk in the woods. Now Chicken Licken was not very clever, so when an acorn fell on his head, he thought that the sky must be falling down. He set off as fast as he could to tell the king. On the way he met Henny Penny and Cocky Locky.

"I am off to tell the king that the sky is falling in," he clucked.

"We will come too," said Henny Penny and Cocky Locky.

So Chicken Licken, Henny Penny and Cocky Locky set off

to find the king. On the way they met Ducky Lucky and Drakey Lakey.

"We are off to tell the king that the sky is falling in," clucked Chicken Licken.

"We will come too," said Ducky Lucky and Drakey Lakey.

So Chicken Licken, Henny Penny, Cocky Locky, Ducky Lucky and Drakey Lakey all set off to find the king. On the way they met Goosey Loosey and Turkey Lurkey.

"We are off to tell the king that the sky is falling in," clucked Chicken Licken.

"We will come too," said Goosey Loosey and Turkey Lurkey.

So Chicken Licken, Henny Penny, Cocky Locky, Ducky Lucky, Drakey Lakey, Goosey Loosey and Turkey Lurkey all set

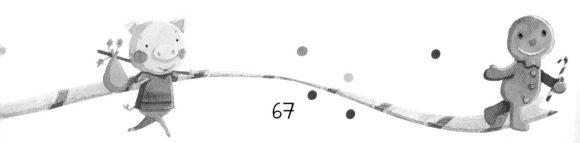

off to find the king. On the way
they met Foxy Loxy.

"We are off to tell the king
that the sky is falling in,"
clucked Chicken Licken.

"What a good thing I met
you all," said Foxy Loxy with

a cunning smile. "I know the way, follow me."

So Chicken Licken, Henny Penny, Cocky Locky, Ducky Lucky, Drakey Lakey, Goosey Loosey and Turkey Lurkey all set off behind Foxy Loxy. He led them all straight to his den, where he planned to eat them all for dinner! But just as he was going to lead them all down into his den, there was a bump, and another acorn fell on Chicken Licken's head.

He looked up and he looked down, and then he said, "That was what fell on my head! It wasn't the sky – it was an acorn!"

Everyone laughed. Then they

all turned round and went
home. Foxy Loxy didn't eat
them all up, and they never got
to visit the king.

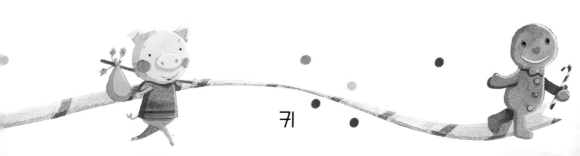

The Three Little Pigs

Once there were three little pigs. One day it was time for them to leave home and make their own way in the world.

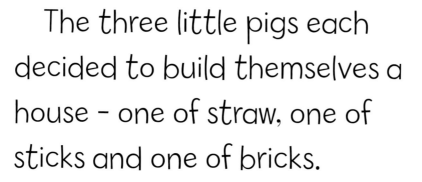

The three little pigs each decided to build themselves a house - one of straw, one of sticks and one of bricks.

They had just finished when along came a big bad wolf. He went up to the straw house.

"Little pig, little pig, let me come in!" shouted the wolf.

"Not by the hair on my chinny chin chin. I'll not let you in," squeaked the first little pig.

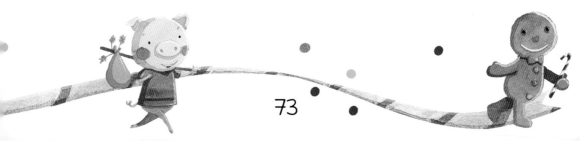

ONCE UPON A TIME

"Then I'll huff and I'll puff, and I'll blow your

house down," shouted the wolf.
And he did. He huffed and he
puffed and he blew the straw
house down.

But the little pig escaped
and ran to the house of sticks.

Then along came the big bad
wolf. He knocked on the door of
the stick house.

"Little pig, little
pig, let me

come in!" shouted the wolf.

"Not by the hair on my chinny chin chin. I'll not let you in," squeaked the second little pig.

"Then I'll huff and I'll puff, and I'll blow your house down," shouted the wolf. And he did. But the two little pigs escaped and ran to the house of bricks.

Along came the big bad wolf.

"Little pig, little pig, let me come in!" shouted the wolf.

"Not by the hair on my chinny chin chin. I'll not let you in," squeaked the third little pig.

"Then I'll huff and I'll puff, and I'll blow your house down," shouted the wolf.

And he tried. He huffed and he puffed but he could not blow the brick house down.

So the wolf climbed onto the roof and down the chimney. But the clever little pigs had placed

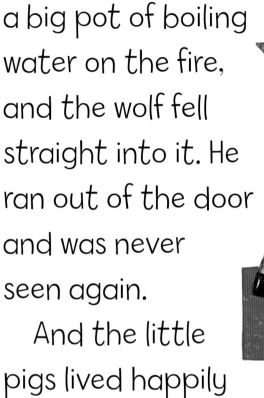

a big pot of boiling water on the fire, and the wolf fell straight into it. He ran out of the door and was never seen again.

And the little pigs lived happily in the brick house.

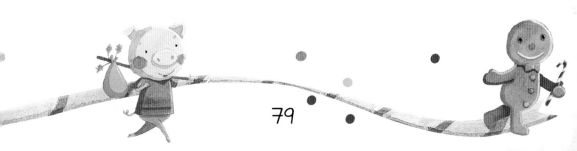

The Elves and the Shoemaker

There was once a shoemaker who was so poor that he only had enough leather left to make one pair of shoes. Before bedtime he cut out the pieces of leather to make the shoes.

Then he said his prayers
and went to bed.

In the morning, when
the shoemaker sat
down to work, he
found the shoes
standing finished
on his table. The
stitching was
beautiful,
and the shoes
were perfect.

He was amazed!

Soon after that, a man came in, and he liked the shoes so much, he paid more than the ordinary price for them. So the shoemaker was able to buy leather for two more pairs of shoes with the money.

He cut them out in the evening, and when he got up the next day, the shoes were finished again, and two more people bought them. That gave the shoemaker so much money that he was able to buy leather for four pairs of shoes.

Early next morning he found the four pairs finished, and so it went on – what he cut out in the evening was finished in the morning. He soon had plenty of money for food, and even enough to buy himself and his wife fine new clothes.

One evening, not long before Christmas, when the shoemaker had cut out his leather as usual, he said to his wife, "How would it be if we were to sit up tonight to see who it is that helps us?"

His wife agreed, so they lit a candle and hid themselves in the corner of the room, behind some clothes that were hanging up there.

At midnight two little men

dressed in rags came in. They sat down at the shoemaker's table, took up the leather, and began with their tiny fingers to stitch, sew and hammer. They did not stop till everything was finished, and then they ran quickly away.

The next day the shoemaker's wife said, "Those little men have made us rich – we ought to say thank you. They must be cold in those rags. I will make them shirts and trousers, and knit them socks, and you can make each of them a pair of shoes."

The shoemaker agreed, and in the evening, when they had everything ready, they laid out the presents on the table, and hid themselves to see how the little men would behave.

At midnight the two little men came skipping in, but, instead of the leather cut out and ready, they found the lovely little clothes.

At first they were surprised,

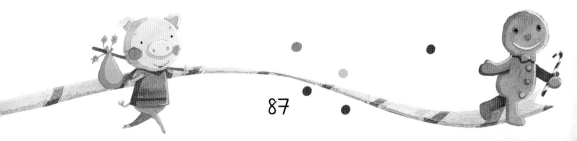

and then very happy.
They put on and
smoothed
down the
pretty little
clothes, singing:
   "Now we're
dressed so fine
and neat,
   Why cut and sew
for others' feet?"
   Then they ran

across the floor and out of the door. They didn't come back any more, but the shoemaker had good luck in everything he did.

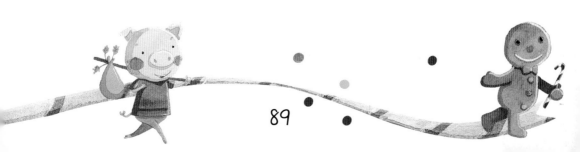

The Wolf and the Seven Little Kids

There was once a goat who had seven little kids. One day she had to go into the wood to fetch food for them, so she said, "Dear children, I am going out and while I am gone, take care that you don't let the wolf in. You'll know it's him by his deep voice and black paws."

"Yes," answered the kids, "we will take good care of ourselves."

It was not long before someone came knocking at the door, saying, "Open the door, dear children. It's Mother and I have a treat for you."

But the little kids said, "You are not our mother. She has a

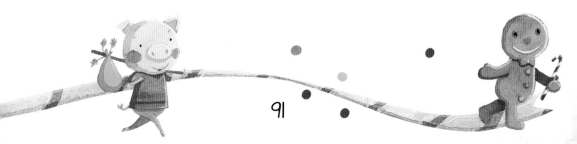

soft and sweet voice. You must be the wolf."

So the wolf went off to a shop and bought a big lump of chalk. He ate it up to make his voice soft. Then he came back, knocked at the door, and said, "Open the door, dear children. Your mother is here, and has brought

something for each of you."

But the wolf had put his black paws up against the window, and the kids said, "We will not open the door. Our mother doesn't have black paws."

So the wolf ran to a baker and got him to cover his paws in white flour. Then he went back to the door and knocked again, showing his paws at the window.

The kids heard the soft voice,

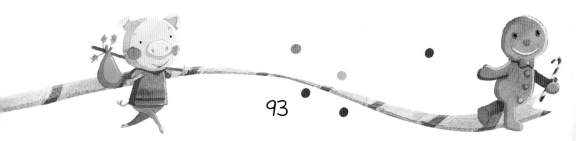

and saw the white paws, so they opened the door.

When they saw it was the wolf they ran to hide. One went under the table, the second got into the bed, the third into the oven, the fourth ran into the kitchen, the fifth into the cupboard, the sixth under the sink, and the seventh into the grandfather clock.

But the wolf found them all,

and one by one he swallowed them down, all except the youngest, because he didn't look inside the grandfather clock. Then the wolf strolled out into the garden and fell asleep.

Not long afterwards, the mother goat came back from the wood, and, oh dear, how she cried to find all her children gone. But she heard the youngest kid calling to her. She

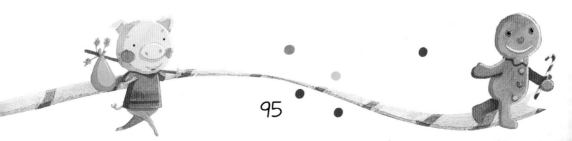

found him in the clock, and he told her what had happened.

The mother goat ran out into the garden, where she saw the wolf lying asleep. She took a huge run at him and butted him with her strong head. *Bang!* Then she kicked him with her strong hooves. *Biff!* She kicked him so

96

hard that all her children came tumbling out of his mouth, one after another. Then she chased him out of her garden.

The mother goat went back to the house with all her children jumping around her. And that big bad wolf never came back again.

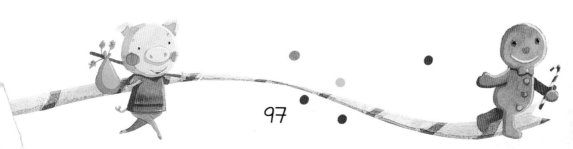

Goldilocks and the Three Bears

One day a little girl called Goldilocks went for a walk in a wood behind her house.

Now, in this wood there lived a family of three bears. The first was a great big bear, the second

was a medium-sized bear, and the third was a teeny-tiny bear. They all lived together in a little house.

When Goldilocks saw the bears' house she wondered who lived there. "I'll just look in and see," she said.

But there was no one there,

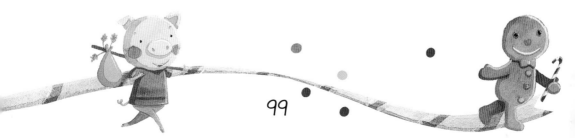

because the bears had all gone out for a walk.

Goldilocks was rather hungry, and when she saw three bowls of porridge on the table, she thought she'd have a taste.

First she tried the porridge in the great big bowl, but that was too hot. Next, she tried the porridge in the medium-sized bowl, but that was too cold. Then she tried the porridge in

the teeny-tiny bowl, and that was just right. It was so good that she ate it all up.

Then Goldilocks decided she wanted a rest. She went over to three chairs standing in a row.

First she tried sitting on the great big chair, but that was too hard. Next, she tried sitting

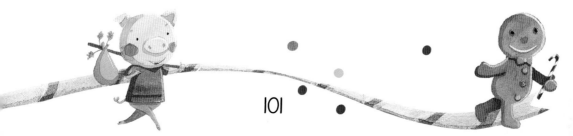

on the medium-sized chair, but that was too soft. Then she tried sitting on the teeny-tiny chair, and that was just right. But when she was getting comfortable, she gave a little wriggle and the chair broke into pieces.

There was a staircase in the

bears' house, and Goldilocks thought she would like to have a look upstairs.

She found a bedroom, and in the middle of the room stood a great big bed. On one side of it there was a medium-sized bed, and on the other side there was a teeny-tiny bed.

Goldilocks was sleepy, so she thought she would lie down and have a little nap.

First she got up on the great big bed, but that was too hard. Next, she tried the medium-sized bed, but that was too soft. Then she tried the teeny-tiny bed, and that was just right, so she fell fast asleep.

While she was sleeping, the three bears came back from their walk. First they looked at the kitchen table.

"Someone has been eating my

porridge!" said the great big bear in a great big voice.

"Someone has been eating my porridge," said the medium-sized bear in a medium-sized voice.

"Someone has been eating *my* porridge, and they've eaten it all up," said the teeny-tiny bear in a teeny-tiny voice.

Next the bears looked at their chairs.

"Someone has been sitting in

my chair!" said the great big bear in a great big voice.

"Someone has been sitting in my chair!" said the medium-sized bear in a medium-sized voice.

"Someone has been sitting in *my* chair, and it's all broken," said the teeny-tiny bear in a teeny-tiny voice.

Then the bears went upstairs.

"Someone has been sleeping in my bed" said the great big bear

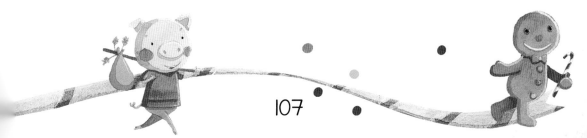

in a great big voice.

"Someone has been sleeping in my bed," said the medium-sized bear in a medium-sized voice.

"Someone has been sleeping in *my* bed, *and she's still in it!*" said the teeny-tiny bear in quite a big voice.

In fact, he said it so loudly that Goldilocks woke up. When she saw the three bears she leapt out of bed and ran down the stairs. And Goldilocks didn't stop running until she was all the way home.

Strange and Silly

The Magic Porridge Pot

Once upon a time there was a little girl, who lived with her mother in a tiny house. They were very poor, and one day they had nothing to eat in the house. So the little girl went into the forest to see if she could find some berries. There, she met an old woman and helped her pick up sticks for her fire.

"Thank you," said the old woman. "You are kind and good. I am a fairy, and in return for your kindness, I will give you this magic porridge pot. If you say, 'Boil, little pot,' it will cook you the most deliciously sweet porridge. When it has made enough porridge, just say, 'Stop, little pot, stop,' and it will stop cooking and clean itself."

The little girl took the pot home, and from then on she and her mother were never hungry.

Whenever they wanted to eat, the little girl simply said "Boil, little pot." Then the pot made as much sweet porridge as they wanted.

One day, the little girl went out, and her mother said, "Boil, little pot!" She ate till she was full, but then she forgot what to say to make the pot stop.

"Stop now!" she said. But the porridge kept coming. "Enough, pot!" she said. But the porridge kept coming.

"Stop, pot, stop!" she said.

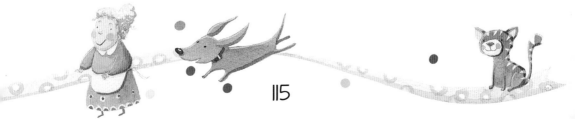

But the porridge kept coming. "Pot, stop, please!" she said. But the porridge kept coming. "Little pot, stop!" she shouted. But the porridge kept coming.

The porridge filled the pot. Then it filled the stove. Next it filled the kitchen. Finally it flowed out of the house and down the road.

At last the little girl came back home, wading through the

porridge to her front door. "Stop, little pot, stop," she shouted.

At once the porridge stopped coming. But now, whoever comes into the village has to paddle through piles of porridge.

The Fish and the Hare

Once upon a time, a poor man was cutting wood in a forest. One of the trees he cut down was hollow, and inside it he found a huge pot full of gold coins! The old man danced for joy. "Hooray!" he cried. "Now we can have food and drink and coals for the winter."

But then he remembered something. His wife loved to talk to people. She always told the whole village everything that happened in their lives.

'If everyone knows about this they will talk and the sheriff will hear,' thought the old man. 'The

sheriff is so greedy he will surely find a way to take our money.'
So the old man made a plan.

The man hid the pot and walked further into the woods. There, he trapped a hare and a fish. He hung the fish at the top of a tree and put the hare in a net in the river. Then he went home and told his wife what he had found.

"A huge pot of gold!" said the

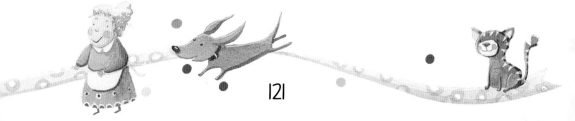

man to his wife. "And we will fetch it together now in our old cart."

They set off to drive through the forest. As they drove the man said, "Do you know, wife, I heard that fish have started to live in trees. And hares now live in the rivers. It's all changed nowadays."

"Is that true?" said his wife, and she started to look around.

Suddenly she said, "Look! There's a fish in that tree there."

They drove on a little further, and then the woman saw the hare. She was too far away to see the net, so she said, "And look, there's a hare in the river. What wonders we have seen!"

After that, the old man and his wife collected the huge pot. They covered it up with sacks and drove home.

Of course, they were very happy to have so much money. But soon, just as the husband knew she would, the wife started to tell everyone about it.

As soon as the greedy sheriff

heard the news, he began to think how he could get the money for himself. So he sent some of his men to the woodcutter's house.

They said that any money found in the forest belonged to the sheriff. The old man just shrugged his shoulders and said, "What money? This is just some story my wife is telling. She tells stories all the time. They're not true. Ask her how we found it."

So the sheriff's men called the man's wife in, and she told them, "Well, we were driving through the forest when we saw a fish up a tree..."

"Fish don't live in trees," said one of the sheriff's men.

"Oh, they do now," said the

wife. "Then we saw a hare swimming in the river."

"This is all nonsense," said another of the sheriff's men. "Sorry we bothered you." And away they went.

So, the old man and his wife got to keep their money and they lived happily ever after.

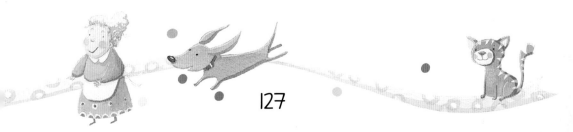

The Stone-cutter's Wishes

Once upon a time, there was a stone-cutter who went every day to a great rock in the side of a mountain. The stone-cutter cut out slabs of rocks for building houses and paths.

One day, he carried some stones to the house of a rich man. The walls were hung with pink silk and silver embroidery. The table had sweets and delicate biscuits on it. The furniture was made of gold and sweet-smelling woods.

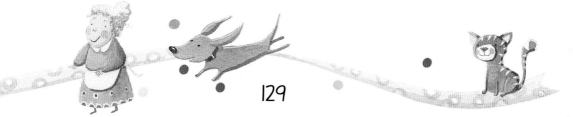

The stone-cutter said to himself, "Oh, if only I were a rich man!" And a voice answered him, "I am the fairy of the mountain. Your wish is granted. You shall be a rich man!"

When the stone-cutter got home, instead of his wooden hut there stood a grand palace. It was filled with beautiful furniture. The bed was stuffed with goose feathers, and the sheets were made of silk.

For a while, the stone-cutter was happy ordering his servants around and enjoying his amazing treasures. But one morning, the stone-cutter saw a beautiful carriage passing by. It was pulled by four white horses with white feather plumes and turquoise reins.

In the carriage sat a prince, dressed in rich clothes. Over the prince's head a servant held a golden umbrella.

"Oh, if only I were a prince!" said the stone-cutter. "Oh, if only I could go in a carriage like that. If I could have a golden umbrella held over me, how happy I would be!"

The voice of the mountain fairy answered, "Your wish is granted. You shall be a prince."

And a prince he became. His

carriage was blue and silver. A servant held a peacock umbrella over his head.

But it was summer, and the sun came into his carriage, making him hot. The stone-cutter looked out of his carriage and saw how the sun dried up the rivers, and he said, "The sun is stronger than I am. Oh, if only I were the sun!"

And the mountain fairy answered, "Your wish is granted. You shall be the sun."

And so the stone-cutter became the sun. He shone down warming the cold earth. But then a cloud covered his face, and hid the earth from him. No matter how he tried, he couldn't shine through it.

He shouted out, "So, a cloud can stop my rays reaching the earth. It must be more important than I am. I wish I were a cloud!"

And the mountain fairy answered, "Your wish is granted. You shall be a cloud!"

And a cloud he became. For weeks the cloud blocked out the sun. He poured out rain till the rivers overflowed their banks, flooding towns and villages.

Only the mountain stayed the same. The cloud said, "The mountain is stronger than I am. Oh, I wish I were the mountain!"

And the mountain fairy answered, "Your wish is granted. You shall be the mountain!"

And the mountain he became. "This is better than everything!" the stone-cutter said to himself.

But one day, along came a stone-cutter. He drove tools into the mountain's surface and hit it with a hammer.

A trembling feeling ran through the mountain. A great block broke off and fell upon the ground. Then he shouted, "An ordinary man can break me into pieces! Oh, if I were only a man!"

And the mountain fairy answered, "Your wish is granted. You shall be a man."

And a man he was once more. He set to work again at his job of stone cutting, and stopped asking for things he had not got. He was happy at last, and he never again heard the voice of the mountain fairy.

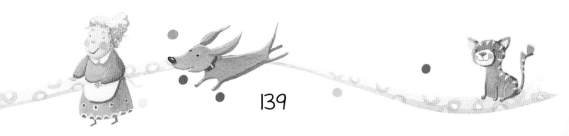

The Enormous Turnip

Once upon a time, an old man planted some turnip seeds. He hoed them and watered them. Then he weeded them, and all the turnips grew well. But one started to grow bigger

than the others.
It grew and it
grew and it grew.
First it was as big
as an apple.
Then it was as
big as a
pumpkin.
Soon, it was even
bigger than the man
himself. It grew so big
that no one could

remember ever seeing such a huge turnip before.

At last it seemed to have stopped growing, and the old man decided it was time to pull it up. He took hold of the leaves and stalk of the great big turnip. He pulled and pulled, but the turnip did not move.

The old man called his wife to come and help him. The old woman put her arms round the

old man, and the old man pulled
the turnip. Together they pulled
and pulled, but the huge turnip
did not move.

So the old woman called her

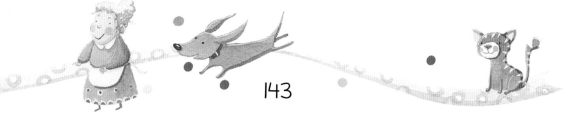

granddaughter to come and help. The granddaughter pulled the old woman. The old woman pulled the old man. The old man pulled the turnip, but still the turnip did not move.

The granddaughter called to the dog to come and help. The dog pulled, the granddaughter pulled, the old woman pulled, and the old man pulled. But the great big turnip did not move.

The dog called to the cat to come and help pull the turnip. The cat pulled, the dog pulled, the granddaughter pulled, the old woman pulled and the old man pulled. Still the turnip did not move.

Then the cat called to a mouse to come and help pull up the great big turnip. Then, the mouse pulled, the cat pulled, the dog pulled, the granddaughter pulled, the old woman pulled and the old man pulled. Together they pulled and pulled, but still the turnip did not move.

Then they all took a deep breath and pulled again, as hard as they could. And suddenly... *pop!*

The great big turnip came out of the ground and everyone tumbled over.

The old man put the turnip in his wheelbarrow and carried it home. Then everyone had turnip for tea, turnip for breakfast and turnip for lunch. In fact, they all had turnip every day for a great many days after that.

The Three Men and the Dream

One day three men were travelling together and got lost. They decided to stay where they were, and sleep under the trees. They only had one small piece of bread to eat and they were all very hungry.

"If we each have a bit," said the first man, "we'll all still be hungry. Let's go to sleep and whoever has the most wonderful dream will get the piece of bread in the morning."

The others agreed, so they put the piece of bread in a box and all lay down and fell asleep. But in the night one of the men, who was a bit of a cheat, got up

and ate the bread. Then he lay
down and went back to sleep.

The night passed, and two of
the men woke up hungry the
next morning. The third man

woke up when he heard his friends talking. He lay still with his eyes shut while he worked out what to tell them. The first two men both wanted to win the piece of bread so one of them started to tell his dream.

"I dreamt a golden host of angels came and took me up to heaven," he said. "There were trumpets blowing and the chief angel waited at the gate to welcome me."

Then it was the turn of the second man. "I too dreamt I went to heaven. In my dream God himself welcomed me and took me to sit near his golden throne. This makes my dream more important than yours, so I win the bread."

The third man pretended to wake up suddenly, and

stared at his two friends. "What! Are you still here?" he cried out. "I dreamt you two had gone up to heaven, and as no one ever comes back from heaven, I got up and ate the bread myself."

King Midas has Ass's Ears

A long time ago in Greece, people believed there were many gods. This story is about King Midas, who had the bad luck to annoy one of the gods.

The god punished King Midas

by giving him a pair of ass's ears. An ass is another word for a donkey, so you can imagine how silly he looked. Instead of his own neat human ears, he had a huge pair of hairy grey ass's ears.

King Midas felt ridiculous, and didn't want anyone to know that he had great big ass's ears. He wore a huge gold crown all through the day to hide them, and never took it off until he went to bed alone at night. But one person did know about the king's ears and that was the man who cut his hair.

The king couldn't hide his ears from his hairdresser! But he made the man promise never to tell anyone his secret. The poor hairdresser really wanted to tell someone about it. But he had promised, and he knew the king would be very angry if he told anyone the secret.

One day the hairdresser almost told one of his friends. Then he started to worry that he might tell someone by accident. So in the end, he came up with an idea. He would tell the story to something that wasn't alive, and that would make him feel better but still keep the secret safe.

The hairdresser walked out of the town into the fields, until he got to the riverbank. He knelt down and dug a hole, and whispered into it, "King Midas has ass's ears."

Then he piled the earth back into the hole. He went back to the town, feeling better.

King Midas' secret remained safe for a while. But one day a bunch of reeds grew up out of the earth in which the hairdresser had dug the hole. Every time the wind blew, the reeds swayed in the wind. As they swayed, they whispered, "King Midas has ass's ears. King Midas has ass's ears..."

As people walked along the river, they heard the whisper in the reeds, and wondered what it meant. They all started whispering to each other, "Have you heard the news? King Midas has ass's ears." Soon the news had spread all around the town.

There was nothing King Midas

could do. Whenever the wind blew, the reeds whispered "King Midas has ass's ears." So the king had to give up and show everyone his ears. The reeds went on whispering their story. And if you listen very carefully to reeds swaying in the wind today, you'll still hear them whispering their secret.

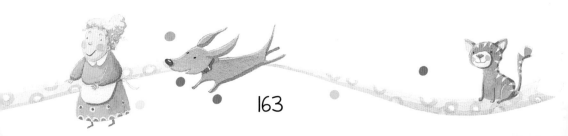

The Three Wishes

There was once an old woman, who was all alone in her cottage one evening. While she was waiting for her husband to return from work, a fine lady came in and asked to borrow her frying pan.

The old woman had never seen her before, but she had a kind heart and so was happy to lend it. Two days later the lady brought it back and said, "Many thanks for lending me this and now in return you shall have three wishes."

And with that she vanished. The old woman was excited about her three wishes, and

began to think about what she
should wish for. In the end, she
thought it would be best to
wait until her husband came
home, so they could decide on
the wishes together.

But then she thought it was a
shame that there were only
hard crusts of bread for her
husband when he came home.
She remembered last time she
had been to her neighbour's

house where the wife had
cooked a fine big sausage.

"Ah, I wish I had that sausage
here!" sighed the old
woman. The next
moment a big
sausage lay on

the table before her.

She was just going to put it in the pan when her husband came in.

"Husband!" cried the woman, "It's all over with our troubles and hard work now. I lent my pan to a fine lady, and she gave me three wishes. The wishes are coming true, for just look at this sausage, which I got the moment I wished for it!"

"What do you mean?" shouted the husband. "Have you wasted a wish on a sausage? You could have had anything in the world. I wish the sausage were sticking to your nose!"

And suddenly there was the sausage, sticking to the woman's nose. She began pulling away at it, but she couldn't get it off.

The husband tried to help his wife to get rid of the sausage.

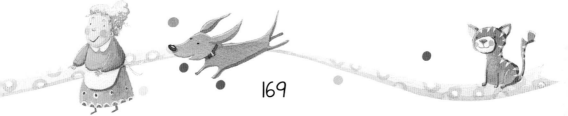

He pulled and tugged, but it
made no difference.

Now they only had one wish
left, and what should they wish
for? They could, of course, wish
for something very fine and
grand, but how could they enjoy
it when the woman had a long
sausage sticking to her nose?

So the husband had to waste
the third and final wish in
wishing the sausage off his wife's

nose. The minute it was gone they were so relieved that they jumped up and danced around the room. For although a sausage may be delicious when you have it in your mouth, it is quite a different thing to have one sticking to your nose for your whole life.

Tikki Tikki Tembo

Once upon a time, in China, there were two brothers. One was called Sam, and the other was called Tikki Tikki Tembo No Sarimbo Hari Kari Bushkie Perry Pem Do Hai Kai Pom Pom

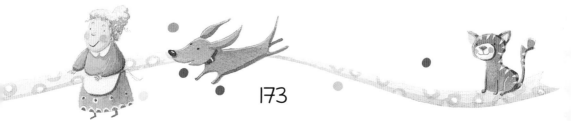

Nikki No Meeno Dom Barako.

One day, the two brothers were playing near the river in their garden when Sam fell into the water. Tikki Tikki Tembo No Sarimbo Hari Kari Bushkie Perry Pem Do Hai Kai Pom Pom Nikki No Meeno Dom Barako ran to his mother, shouting, "Quick, Sam has fallen into the river."

"What?" cried the mother, "Sam has fallen into the river?

Run and tell Father!"

Together they ran to the father and said, "Quick, Sam has fallen into the river. What shall we do?"

"Sam has fallen into the river?" said the father. "Run and tell the gardener!"

Then they all ran to the gardener and shouted, "Quick, Sam has fallen into the river. What shall we do?"

"Sam has fallen into the river?" cried the gardener, and he quickly fetched a rope. He rescued Sam, who was wet and cold and frightened, and ever so happy to still be alive.

Sometime afterwards the two brothers were again

playing near the river. This time Tikki Tikki Tembo No Sarimbo Hari Kari Bushkie Perry Pem Do Hai Kai Pom Pom Nikki No Meeno Dom Barako fell into the river.

Sam ran to his mother, shouting, "Quick, Tikki Tikki Tembo No Sarimbo Hari Kari Bushkie Perry Pem Do Hai Kai Pom Pom Nikki No Meeno Dom Barako has fallen into the river. What shall we do?"

"What?" cried the mother, "Tikki Tikki Tembo No Sarimbo Hari Kari Bushkie Perry Pem Do Hai Kai Pom Pom Nikki No Meeno Dom Barako has fallen into the river? Run and tell Father!"

Together they ran to the father and cried, "Quick, Tikki Tikki Tembo No Sarimbo Hari Kari Bushkie Perry Pem Do Hai Kai Pom Pom Nikki No Meeno Dom Barako has fallen into the river.

What shall we do?"

"Tikki Tikki Tembo No Sarimbo Hari Kari Bushkie Perry Pem Do Hai Kai Pom Pom Nikki No Meeno Dom Barako has fallen into the river?" cried the father. "Run and tell the gardener!"

Then they all ran to the gardener and shouted, "Quick, Tikki Tikki Tembo No Sarimbo Hari Kari Bushkie Perry Pem Do Hai Kai Pom Pom Nikki No Meeno

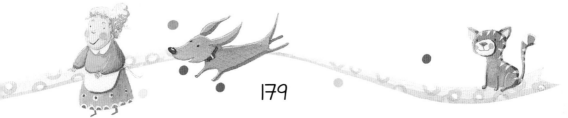

Dom Barako has fallen into the river. What shall we do?"

"Tikki Tikki Tembo No Sarimbo Hari Kari Bushkie Perry Pem Do Hai Kai Pom Pom Nikki No Meeno Dom Barako has fallen into the river?" cried the gardener.

Then he quickly fetched a rope and pulled Tikki Tikki Tembo No Sarimbo Hari Kari Bushkie Perry Pem Do Hai Kai Pom Pom Nikki No Meeno Dom Barako out of the river. However, the poor boy had been in the water so long that he had very nearly drowned.

And from that time on, the Chinese have given their children short names.

The Stars in the Sky

Once upon a time, there was a girl who wanted to climb up to the stars in the sky and play among them. So one day she set out to find them.

She walked and she walked

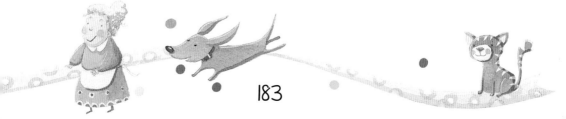

until she came to a bubbling brook. "Good day to you, Brook," she said. "I'm looking for the stars in the sky to play with. Have you seen them?"

"Yes, indeed, my bonny lassie," said the brook. "They glint in my water at night. Paddle about, and maybe you'll find one."

So the girl paddled and paddled, but

she didn't find the stars in the water. So the girl walked on until she came to the fairies dancing. "Good day to you, Good People," she said. "I'm looking for the stars in the sky to play with. Can you help me?"

"Why, yes," they said. "They shine on the grass at night. Dance with us here, and maybe they'll come to you."

So the girl took hands with the fairies and danced and danced and danced. But the stars didn't come down, and she sat down in the grass and burst into tears.

"Oh deary me, oh deary me," she said. "I've paddled and I've danced, and if you won't help me I shall never find the stars in the sky to play with."

But the Good Folk whispered together. Then one of them took the girl by the hand and said, "If you won't go home to your mother, go forward. Mind you take the right road. Ask Four Feet to carry you to No Feet at all. Then tell No Feet at all to carry you to the stairs without steps, and if you can climb that—"

The little girl didn't

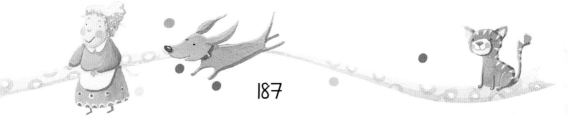

understand, but she walked on until she came to a horse tied to a tree.

"You must be Four Feet!" she said. "Will you carry me to the stars in the sky?"

"No," said the horse, "I don't know anything about the stars in the sky, and I'm here to do the orders of the Good Folk, and not what I want."

"Well," said the little girl, "I've

come from the Good Folk, and they told me to tell Four Feet to carry me to No Feet at all."

"Well, that's different," said the horse. "Jump up and ride on my back!"

So they rode till they got out of the forest and found themselves at the edge of the sea.

On the water in front of them was a wide glistening path. It ran straight out towards a beautiful arch, which rose out of the water and went up into the sky. It was all the colours in the world, and wonderful to look at.

"Now get you down," said the horse. "I've brought you to the end of the land, and that's as much as Four Feet can do. I must go away home now."

So the little girl climbed down from the horse and stood at the edge of the water. Suddenly a strange fish came swimming right up to her feet.

"Good day to you, Big Fish," the girl said. "I'm looking for the stars in the sky, and for the stairs that climb up to them. Will you show me the way?"

"No," said the fish, "I can't

unless you bring me word from the fairies."

"Well," said she, "the fairies said No Feet at all would carry me to the stairs without steps."

"Ah, well," said the fish, "that's all right then. Get on my back and hold tight."

And off the fish went into the water, along the silver path and towards the bright arch.

As they came to

the foot of the arch, the little girl saw it was a broad bright road, sloping up and away into the sky. At the far end of it she could see small shining things dancing about.

"Now," said the fish, "here you are, and there's the stair. Climb up, if you can, but hold on tight," and off he splashed through the water.

So the little girl climbed and she climbed. She felt dizzy in the light, and shivered with the cold, but still she climbed the stair towards the faraway stars that she could see twinkling and dancing at the top.

But the little girl was so tired, that suddenly she slipped, and she fell down, down, down off the stair.

And *bang!* The little girl woke up in her bed at home, and just at that moment, she heard her

mother coming in to her room
to wake her up for her
breakfast.

Icarus, the Flying Boy

Icarus lived long ago on an
island in Greece. He and his
father had come to do some
work for the king of the island,
but then the king got annoyed
with them and would not let

them leave.

They could walk around the island, but they could not go home. They wanted to escape, but there were no boats and the island was too far from other land to swim.

Icarus's father liked making things, and he was very clever. One day, he had an idea. He told his son to collect all the feathers he could find, and he went to the bees' nest to find some wax.

Icarus spent days collecting feathers from all over the island. When he had collected plenty, his father started working.

He heated the wax until it was

a little soft, then he stuck hundreds of feathers into it to make a great big pair of wings.

"Icarus!" he said. "We are going to fly off this island." He made a second pair of wings, and they tied them onto their arms and practised flying.

Icarus jumped into the air, flapping his arms hard, and started to rise. He dipped one wing slightly and found he could turn. Icarus flapped harder, and flew up higher and higher, just like a bird. He could fly!

"Now we will fly off this island," said his father. "But there are two things you must remember. Don't go too low, or the salt spray from the waves will make the feathers wet. And don't go too high or the sun will melt the wax off the feathers."

Together Icarus and his father

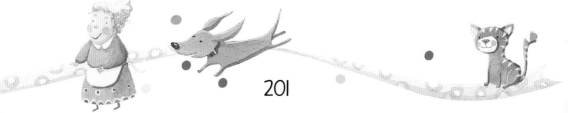

flew off from a high cliff. Icarus's father flew steadily straight, heading for the land far ahead.

But Icarus loved flying. He flew up, he flew down, he flew next to the birds and he flew in great big circles. It was such fun.

Icarus was having such a good time he forgot what his father had said. He flew low and he flew high and then he thought he'd try flying very high - far above

his father.

"Take care!" shouted his father, but it was too late. Icarus flew far too close to the sun, and the wax began melting down his arms. His feathers started dropping off and Icarus fell down, down, down.

Soon all the feathers were gone. Icarus tried flapping just his arms, but everyone knows that doesn't work.

Splash! Icarus landed in the sea and had to swim the rest of the way. He was very cold and tired by the time he reached his father on land.

"Next time," he said, "I'll do what I'm told."

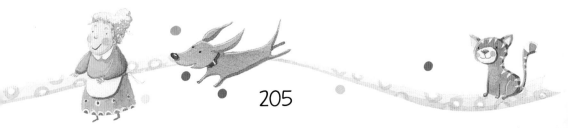

Animal Antics

The Hare and the Tortoise

The hare was always talking about how fast he could run. All the other animals were fed up of his boasting.

One day the hare went out for a stroll, and on his way he

spotted the tortoise. The hare stretched his long legs and thumped the ground with his strong paws. "I am the fastest animal," he said. "No one can beat me."

The wrinkled tortoise poked his head out of his shell and said quietly, "I know I can't run very fast, but I will try to beat you."

"That's a good joke!" said the hare. "I could dance around you the whole way and still win."

"Keep your boasting till you've won," said the tortoise. "Shall we race then?"

So they worked out where they would run and lined up. The other animals shouted "Go!"

The tortoise started off slowly, plodding his way

forwards. The hare ran as fast as he could go, and raced out of sight almost at once. He was soon so far ahead that he decided to stop running and have a little rest. After a mid-morning snack, he was soon fast asleep.

The tortoise plodded on and on, moving slowly but never stopping, and never giving up.

Suddenly, the hare woke up – and saw the tortoise near the finish line! He jumped up and ran as fast as he could go. His strong legs pounded along, but he

could not reach the end in time to beat the tortoise.

The hare was well behind when the tortoise crossed the finish line – he had won the race!

As all the animals cheered, the tortoise smiled quietly and said, "Slow and steady wins the race!"

Why the Dog and Cat are Enemies

Once upon a time there was a husband and wife who lived in a town in China. They didn't have much money, but they always managed to get by because the wife had a gold ring. The ring was magic, and whoever owned it would always have good luck.

However, the husband and wife didn't know this, so they didn't look after the ring. One day, a woman who had come to visit them saw it lying on the windowsill, and quietly slipped it into her pocket.

After that, all the luck went out of the house and the husband and wife grew poorer and poorer. The husband lost his job, so no money came into the house, and they both became very hungry.

Now, the husband and wife had a dog and a cat, and one night the two animals got together and started talking about what they could do to

help their owners.

"We must get the ring back," the dog said.

The cat replied, "I know where it is. I heard the woman who took it talking. It's in a house on the other side of the river, on the far side of town. The ring has been locked in a chest, where no one can get at it."

"You must catch a mouse," said the dog, "and the mouse

must gnaw a hole in the chest and fetch the ring."

The cat liked this idea, so she caught a mouse and the mouse agreed to help. Then the cat, the dog and the mouse set off to walk across town to the river.

The cat could not swim, so when they got to the river, she held the mouse carefully

in her mouth and the dog swam across the river with the cat and the mouse on his back. Then the cat carried the mouse to the house in which the chest stood. The mouse got in through a window, then she gnawed a hole in the chest and brought out the ring.

The cat thanked the mouse and let her go, then she went back to the dog. The dog swam across the river with the cat on

his back. Then they started out for home, to bring the ring back to their owners.

But the dog could only run along the ground – when there was a fence or a house in the way he always had to go around it. The cat, however, could climb up and over things, so she got home long before the dog, and gave the ring to her master.

Her master said to his wife,

"What a good animal the cat is! Look, she has rescued our ring. We will always give her enough to eat and care for her as though she were our own child."

But when the dog came home they had no friendly word for him. "Look what the cat has done!" they said. "Why aren't you more like the cat? Why didn't you help us get the ring,

like the cat?"
The cat sat
by the fireplace
and didn't say
a word. Then
the dog grew
angry at the

cat, because she had taken all the praise for finding the ring.

And ever since that day, the dog and the cat are enemies, and when the dog sees the cat, he tries to chase her. But the dog doesn't usually catch the cat, because she can climb and he can't.

When the Animals got Scared

A long time ago there was a nervous little mouse who lived in a jungle. One day, he was sitting on a rock when a nut fell off a tree above him. The mouse heard the noise the nut made as it hit the rock. He jumped up and started to run away in fright.

The rabbits saw him and said, "Why are you running?"

And the mouse said, "There was a loud noise!" So the rabbits started to run too.

The monkeys saw the rabbits running and asked, "Why are

you running?"

And the rabbits said, "There was a loud noise!" So the monkeys started running.

The gazelles saw the monkeys running and asked, "Why are you running?"

And the monkeys said, "There was a loud noise!" So the gazelles started running.

The jackals saw the gazelles running and asked, "Why are

you running?"

And the gazelles said, "There was a loud noise!" So the jackals started running.

The rhinos saw the jackals running and asked, "Why are you running?"

And the jackals said, "There was a loud noise!" So the rhinos started running.

The elephants saw the rhinos running and asked, "Why are

you running?"

And the rhinos said, "There was a loud noise!" So the elephants started running. And they ran all the way to the place where the lion lived.

The lion asked, "Why are you running?" And the elephants said, "There was a loud noise!"

The lion said, "Show me where the noise came from."

So the elephants walked back

and pointed to the rhinos, and said, "They told us about it."

Then the rhinos pointed to the jackals, the jackals pointed

to the gazelles, the gazelles pointed to the monkeys, the monkeys pointed to the rabbits, the rabbits pointed to the mouse, and finally the mouse led the way into the forest and pointed to the nut.

Everyone looked at the nut and then the lion said to them all, "Next time, before you start to run, look for yourself first to see if there's anything to be afraid of."

The Stupid Crocodiles

Long, long ago, when all the animals could talk, a little white hare lived on a tiny island. The hare was bored and wanted very much to visit the mainland. Day after day he would go out and sit on the shore, and day after day he hoped to find some way of getting across.

One day he saw a crocodile swimming near the island.

'This is lucky!' thought the hare. 'I will ask the crocodile to carry me across the sea!'

But the hare knew that crocodiles were grumpy and dangerous, and he didn't think the crocodile would agree to do what he wanted. So he thought that he would try to get what he wanted by a trick.

He said, "Oh, Mr Crocodile, isn't it a lovely day?"

The crocodile was bored too, so he came over to say hello. He rather liked eating hare, but he wasn't hungry at that moment, so he just said, "What are you doing here?"

The hare said, "Why don't you stop and talk with me for a little while?"

The crocodile came out of the sea and sat on the shore with the

hare. They talked together for some time about this and that.
But all the time the hare was planning how he could use the crocodile to get off the

island and to the mainland.

After a while, the hare said, "Mr Crocodile, I don't know much about crocodiles. You are so big and so strong, there must only be a few of you. Tell me, do you think there are more crocodiles or more hares in the world?"

"Of course there are more crocodiles than hares," answered the crocodile crossly. "Can't you see that for yourself? We live all over the sea. If I called together all the crocodiles who are just in this part of a sea, you could see how many of us there are!"

"That is a sight I would love to see! Please do call them," said the clever hare, "and I will count them when they come!"

The crocodile swam off, and after a little while he came back with a large number of other crocodiles – they looked like floating logs on the waves.

"Look, Mr Hare!" announced the crocodile proudly. "Did you ever see so many crocodiles?"

The hare jumped up and down, clapped his paws together and said, "That is wonderful!"

He pretended to try and count them. "One, two, three... Oh no! I've counted that one twice. One, two, three four... Oh, I can't count you all when you're jumbled together like that. Please could you make a line from this beach to the mainland. I will walk on your backs and count as I go, then I will know exactly how many of you there are."

"All right, but be quick!" said the crocodile, who was beginning to feel like having hare for tea.

The crocodiles organized themselves into a long line, and the hare hopped off the island onto the strange bridge of crocodiles, counting as he jumped from one lumpy, green crocodile to the next.

"Please keep quite still, or I

shall not be able to count," said the hare. "One, two, three, four, five, six, seven, eight, nine... Oh, this is much better."

And the clever hare walked across the crocodile bridge to the mainland. Then he ran off, leaving the crocodiles feeling stupid and hungry.

Where are the Kittens?

Alice and Mark's cat had had three kittens. They were funny and pretty, and Alice and Mark loved playing with them. One was black and white, one was ginger and one was tabby.

The kittens played around their mother's feet all day long, getting into all sorts of mischief and play-fighting with each other. When they were tired they curled up together and slept.

One day, Mark and Alice went out with their

mummy, leaving the kittens in the kitchen with the mother cat. After a good walk, Mark and Alice came in hungry for their tea, but the minute they came in through the door, they knew that something was wrong.

"What's happened?" said Mummy, looking worried.

The kitchen was in a mess and the mother cat was walking up and down, meowing sadly. All sorts of things were all over the floor – a basket, some papers, a soft toy rabbit and some apples. The worst thing was that the three kittens were nowhere to be seen. Where were the kittens?

"Oh, Mummy," said Alice, "something is wrong. Look, there's things all over the floor and the kittens are missing. What's happened to them? Do

you think a fox might have got in and carried them off?"

"I wouldn't think so," said Mummy, looking worried, "but it does look as if something big has been in here and messed around – look at that basket on the floor and those papers."

All this time the mother cat was meowing and meowing.

"I know you're worried," Mark told her. "We're worried too. We

don't know where your kittens
are, but we'll try and find them."

"Alice, go and see if a window
is open," said Mummy. "I'll look
in the garden. Mark, will you pick
the things up off the floor?"

Mark started to tidy the
kitchen. If the kittens had got
outside, they might be lost, and
how would they know how to
come home again?

He picked up the basket and

suddenly he gave a shout.
Mummy and Alice came running
and they all looked at the floor.

There, curled up in a tight
bundle where the basket had
been, were the three kittens.

"I found the kittens," said Mark, "and I think I found who made the mess, too."

The Little Red Hen and the Wheat

Once there was a little red hen. She found a grain of wheat in the barnyard and said, "Who will plant this wheat?"

"I won't," said the dog.

"I won't," said the cat.

"I won't," said the goose.

"I won't," said the turkey.

"I will, then," said the little red hen. "Ca-ca-ca-ca-ca-ca-ca-ca-daa-cut!"

So she planted the grain of wheat.

The sun shone and the rain fell, and the wheat grew until it had a big head of ripe grain at the top.

"Who will cut this wheat?"

The Little Red Hen and the Wheat

said the little red hen.

"I won't," said the dog.

"I won't" said the cat.

"I won't" said the goose.

"I won't," said the turkey.

"I will, then," said the little red hen. "Ca-ca-ca-ca-ca-ca-ca-ca-daa-cut!"

So she cut the wheat.

"Who will thresh the grain out of this wheat?" said the little red hen.

"I won't," said the dog.

"I won't," said the cat.

"I won't," said the goose.

"I won't," said the turkey.

"I will, then," said the little red hen. "Ca-ca-ca-ca-ca-ca-ca-ca-daa-cut!"

So she threshed the wheat.

"Who will take this wheat to the mill to have it ground?" said the little red hen.

"I won't," said the dog.

"I won't" said the cat.

"I won't," said the goose.

"I won't," said the turkey.

"I will, then," said the little

red hen." Ca-ca-ca-ca-ca-ca-ca-ca-daa-cut!"

So she took the wheat to the mill, and by and by she came back with the flour.

"Who will bake this flour?" said the little red hen.

"I won't," said the dog.

"I won't," said the cat.

"I won't," said the goose.

"I won't," said the turkey.

"I will, then," said the little red

hen." Ca-ca-ca-ca-ca-ca-ca-ca-daa-cut!"

So she baked the flour and made a loaf of bread.

"Who will eat this bread?" said the little red hen.

"I will," said the dog.

"I will," said the cat.

"I will," said the goose.

"I will," said the turkey.

"I will," said the little red hen. "Ca-ca-ca-ca-ca-ca-ca-ca-daa-cut!"

And she ate the loaf of bread up all by herself.

The Lion and the Mouse

One day, a lion was sleeping in a jungle clearing when a mouse ran over his paws. Quick as a flash, the lion caught the mouse, trapping her under one of his giant paws. Then the lion

opened his mouth wide to
gobble her up.

"Please let me go!"
cried the little mouse
quickly. "If you do, I
shall never forget
it. And who
knows, one day
I may even
be able to

help you in return."

The lion thought the idea of the little mouse ever being able to help him was so funny that it made him feel kind. So he lifted up his giant paw and let the mouse go.

"Go on, then," he said. "I won't eat you this time."

And still smiling at the idea of a mouse ever being able to help him, the king of the beasts, the

lion went back
to sleep.
    When the lion
awoke, he got up and went out
to hunt. Prowling down a jungle

path, he walked into a trap, and a strong net made of ropes landed on top of him.

The lion struggled to free himself, but as he wriggled and squirmed he became more entangled in the ropes. He found he couldn't get free from the net.

The lion realized the hunter would return to the trap soon, but he was so exhausted he could only lie still and roar softly. As he lay there, unable to move, the little mouse happened to pass by. She saw the lion tied up and ran to help.

With her sharp little teeth she nibbled away at the ropes until one by one they fell away. Then the lion scrambled to his feet and gave a mighty shake. "Thank you," he growled.

"Wasn't I right?" said the

little mouse. "Sometimes even the smallest animal can help the king of the beasts."

And the grateful lion agreed that she was right.

Cat and Copy-cat

One winter day, Grandma had been visiting Mrs Brown in the next village. In the afternoon she started walking home along the road.

The sun was warm and the

snow was packed hard, so it wasn't difficult to walk. Grandma liked the cold, crisp air. She liked the blue sky, and the hills and fields that were white with snow. She liked to hear the birds calling among the trees.

Grandma was halfway home, when she heard a noise behind her. It was, "Meow, meow."

"That sounds like a cat," said Grandma to herself.

"Meow, meow," came the sound again.

This time Grandma looked around. What do you think she saw? There, in the road behind her, were two black-and-white kittens. They were trotting along side by side and they looked just alike.

Grandma stopped and called, "Kitty, kitty, kitty! Where did you come from? Are you following me?"

As soon as Grandma stopped, the kittens stopped too. They sat in the snow and looked at Grandma. She walked back a little way towards them. As she did, the kittens turned and ran

away down the road, then sat down again. They didn't want to be caught.

Grandma called to them again. "Don't be scared, little cats. I'm not going to hurt you. I just want to give you a little stroke and see you're all right."

She tried in every way to get near them, but she could not. Every time she walked towards them, they ran back a bit before they sat down again.

At last, Grandma said, "Poor kittens! You don't know that I'm your friend. I don't like to leave you here in the cold, but I can't stay any longer. It will be starting to get dark soon, and I must go home."

So she walked on up the road. When the kittens saw this, they started after her. Grandma looked back and saw them

following, their little tails
pointed straight up.

"Well, I never!" said Grandma
to herself. "Now, do you suppose
they will follow me home?"

She kept looking back to see. Every time she looked, the kittens were coming. But if she stopped, they stopped.

At last they reached Grandma's house. She opened the gate, walked up the path to her front door and stopped to find her key. The kittens followed her through the gate and along the path, but they stopped halfway along when Grandma

stopped at the door. Grandma turned to look at them.

"Now," she said, "you have followed me to my door. Are you looking for a new home? Did you pick me out? If you really want to live with me, you can."

Grandma unlocked the door and went in. She left the door open, and after a little pause the two black-and-white kittens went in after her.

Grandma found some milk and heated it a little by the fire. Then she put it down, and the kittens ran up close and started to drink.

When the kittens
had finished the
milk, they took a
walk around the
room, sniffing at the
chairs and tables,
and putting out
their little paws to
pat the curtains
and the soft rugs.
Grandma was able to take a
close look at them, at last.

"You are funny kittens," said Grandma. "You are almost alike. You have a black spot on this leg. And you don't. If you are going to be my kittens, I must give you both a name. You are so very nearly alike, I shall call you Cat and Copy-cat. And, if you are good, you shall live with me always."

Well, the kittens were good, and they stayed with Grandma

and kept her company. And every night they curled up together and slept on her bed.

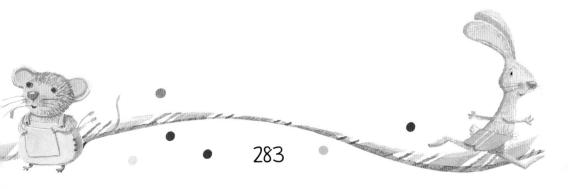

The Lion and the Two Cunning Little Jackals

Once upon a time, in a great jungle, there lived a mighty lion. He was king of all the country round about. Every day he used to leave his den, and roar with a loud, angry voice.

And when the lion roared, the other animals in the jungle got very frightened, and ran here and there. But the lion would pounce upon them, and gobble them up for his dinner.

This went on for a long time, until the only animals left in the jungle were two little jackals, who were husband and wife.

The little jackals would run this way and that to escape the terrible lion. They were always sure they were going to be caught, and every day the lady jackal would say to her husband, "I am afraid he will catch us today. Oh dear, oh dear!"

And her husband would answer her, "Don't be afraid. We'll run on a mile or two. Come on - quick, quick, quick!"

And they would both run away as fast as they could.

One fine day the lion was so close behind them that they could not escape.

Then the male jackal said, "Wife! I feel very frightened. The lion is so angry and he is sure to catch us now. What can we do?"

"Cheer up," his wife replied. "We can save ourselves. I have a plan." And she whispered something to her husband, and he nodded and smiled.

The lion roared and said, "How dare you try and escape me! Come here and be eaten, for I am the king of the jungle."

The cunning little jackals stopped running. They went up to the lion and said, "We know you are strong, but there is a much bigger lion than you

in this jungle. He tried to catch us, and he frightened us so much that we ran away."

"What do you mean?" said the lion. "I am the only lion in the jungle. Show me this other lion so I can fight him."

So the cunning little jackals took him to a place where there was a well dug in the jungle.

The lion looked down into the well, and he thought he saw another lion there. Of course, it was only his reflection in the water, but he didn't understand that. He roared and shook his great mane. Then, when his reflection roared back, he jumped into the well to try and get at the other lion.

Splash! He landed in the water at the bottom. And the sides of the well were so steep that he could not get out again.

So the cunning little jackals ran away, safe and sound, and the terrible lion never hurt anyone ever again.

The Town Mouse and the Country Mouse

Once upon a time, a town mouse went to visit his cousin in the country.

The country mouse was pleased to see him. She showed off her home inside a tree trunk.

It was simple, but warm and cosy. She brought the town mouse some fresh rainwater in an acorn cup, and some grains of corn and berries for dinner. Then she showed him where he could sleep, on a bed of soft sheep's wool she had collected from thorn bushes.

The country mouse took her cousin for walks around the fields, and they met her friends

- the squirrel, the shrew, the dormouse and the mole.

When it rained, they sat inside the country mouse's doorway, and looked out at the rain coming down. When the sun shone, they sat in its warmth, on a sunny bank, and watched the cows in the meadow and the larks in the sky.

The town mouse was very polite and said thank you for

everything, but after a few days he got a little bored.

"You should come and visit me!" he said. "I'd like to show you what my home is like. I sleep on silk sheets, and live inside a large house. I drink

wine, and eat sweet cake and delicious cheese. Come and visit me. You will love it. I don't expect you'll ever want to go home again."

The country mouse agreed to go with her cousin, and the two mice crept into a cart that was going back to town.

The town mouse lived in a grand house in the middle of town. The country mouse was amazed. The pair jumped into a basket of food that was going to be carried into the house.

The basket was put

down in the kitchen. The mice wriggled out, ran across the floor and under a door to the dining room. The entrance to the town mouse's home was a hole in the skirting board.

The town mouse took his cousin into his home and showed her his bed made of handkerchiefs, and his sitting room, kitchen and larder.

"Have some fruit

cake," he said. "Or what about some bits of bacon? Or shall we go and see what the people in the house had for dinner? Let's do that – then you can see how I feast every day." He led his cousin out of the hole into the dining room. "Climb up the tablecloth," he said, scrambling up himself.

On the table, they found a delicious-looking feast. There

were sandwiches and pies, cakes and biscuits – everything that was good to eat. The mice helped themselves.

"Isn't this better than grains of corn?

Don't you think the town is better than the country?" the town mouse said.

"Perhaps..." said the country mouse. "What's that noise?"

"Oh, that's the cat in the kitchen, meowing," said the town mouse. "He can't get in unless someone opens the door."

"Cat?" said the country mouse. "I... I think I'd like to get down now."

"Oh, all right," said the town mouse, and he led the way across the table.

"Mind that," he said, pointing to a strange thing on the floor below them that was made of wire and wood.

"What is it?" asked the country mouse.

"A trap," said the town mouse.

The country mouse began to feel very nervous.

Suddenly, the mice heard growling and scratching at the door. It burst open and two

dogs came bouncing in, sniffing
the air. The dogs began to bark,
jumping up at the table.

"Run!" squeaked the town
mouse, and the mice scampered

away in fear. They climbed down the tablecloth, ran across the floor and back into the town mouse's hole.

"That was awful!" said the country mouse.

"That?" said the town mouse. "No, that was exciting. It makes life fun to be chased once in a while, don't you think? And didn't you like the food?"

"I did like the food," said the

country mouse, "but I like my grains of corn and berries, too. And I like living in a tree trunk, and seeing the sun come up. And best of all, I like feeling safe and comfortable.

"Your town life is very grand, but it's not for me," said the country mouse. "Thank you for having me, but I think I'll go home now."

So the country mouse said

goodbye to her cousin and left the town at once. She jumped on a cart and travelled home, slipping down from the cart as she came to her tree trunk.

The country mouse sat down, looking at the buttercups in the sunshine. She was very happy to think that she was back in her comfortable little home.

"It is better to live a simple life in peace," she said to herself, "than a rich life in danger."

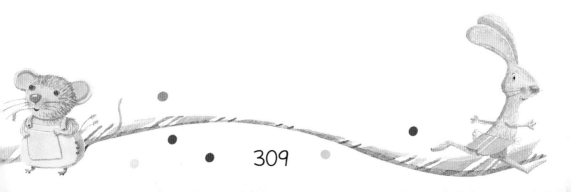

Tricks and Teases

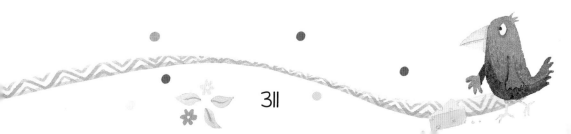

Why the Bear is Stumpy-tailed

Once upon a time, there was a bear who lived in a cold country. In those days, the bear had a beautiful long tail, and he was very proud of it. One day, the bear was out on the ice, and

he met a fox. The fox had a string of fish that he'd just stolen from a fisherman.

The bear saw the fish, and said, "Where did you get those fish, Fox?"

The fox said, "I caught them. I've been out fishing in the ice."

So the bear said, "Can I have some of your fish?"

The fox loved to play tricks, and, as he was jealous of the bear's tail, he said, "No, you can't have my fish, but I'll teach you to catch your own fish instead. Would you like that?"

"Oh yes!" replied the bear. "I would love to learn how to fish."

So the fox said, "Here's what you must do. First, make a hole

in the ice, then stick your tail in
the hole. It will feel cold, but
don't worry, you'll get used to it.
Just keep your tail in the ice.

"It will start to hurt,"
continued the fox, "but that's
just the fish nibbling at your
tail. Hold very still so you don't
scare the fish away.

"After a bit your tail will start
to feel heavy," the fox went on.
"When it feels like that, jump up

suddenly so you pull your tail out of the water, and you'll have lots of fish on it."

So the bear made a hole in the ice. Then he lowered his tail into the water. It was so cold!

The bear held very still, and after a while his tail started to ache with the cold. He felt as if sharp needles were pricking him.

"It's the fish," the bear said to himself. "The fish are nibbling!

Oh, I am going to have so many fish to eat." He kept still.

After a while, his tail felt very heavy. (This was really because the ice had closed up around his tail, not because there were lots of fish hanging off it.)

"Time to jump up and get the fish," said the bear. He jumped up as quickly as he could to pull his tail out of the icy water. But the bear's tail had been in the water for so long it was frozen into the ice. When the bear jumped up, he pulled his tail right off!

"Ow! Ow! Ow!" he yelped.
And that's why the bear and
the fox are enemies, and why
the bear has a stumpy tail.

The Fox and the Crow

A fox once saw a crow fly off with a piece of cheese in its beak. The crow settled on the branch of a tree.

"That's going to be my cheese," said Mr Fox to himself,

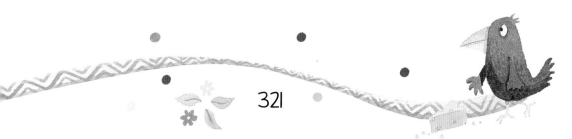

and he walked up to the tree. "Good day, Mrs Crow," cried Mr Fox. "How well you are looking today. How shiny your feathers are, and how bright your eyes." The crow cocked her head and listened happily. "I'm sure you must sing beautifully, too," Mr Fox went on. "If I could only hear you

322

sing, I would be completely happy."

And so Mrs Crow lifted up her head and began to caw her loudest. But, of course, the moment she opened her mouth to sing, the cheese fell straight to the ground.

Snap! Mr Fox gobbled up the

piece of cheese.

"That will do," said Mr Fox with a grin. "That was all I wanted. In exchange for your tasty cheese I will give you a piece of advice for the

future, Mrs Crow – do not trust flatterers."

And with that he walked away, licking his lips.

Brer Rabbit and the Tar Baby

Brer Rabbit and Brer Fox were enemies. Brer Fox was always trying to catch Brer Rabbit, but Brer Rabbit was just too clever to be caught.

One day, Brer Fox thought up

a new plan to catch Brer Rabbit.
He made a sticky black model of
a baby out of tar, and left it
sitting by the road.

Soon Brer Rabbit
came hopping
along and spotted
the little figure.
"Good morning!"
he said,
cheerily.
The Tar Baby

said nothing.

"Good morning!" Brer Rabbit said again, crossly.

The Tar Baby said nothing.

"Where are your manners?" said Brer Rabbit, angrily.

Still the Tar Baby said nothing. Brer Rabbit felt so cross, he reached across to give the Tar Baby a tap on the arm. But as soon as his paw touched the tar, it stuck there! He couldn't pull it away. So Brer Rabbit tried to use his other paw to pull it free, and that got stuck too. Next, Brer Rabbit brought up his strong back legs to kick himself free but they got stuck as well. So there Brer Rabbit was, stuck to the Tar Baby, and that was when Brer Fox strolled up.

"I've caught you at last, Brer Rabbit!" Brer Fox cried. "Now, what shall I do with you?"

"Oh please," said Brer Rabbit, "do anything you want with me, but don't throw me in the briar patch." Brer Rabbit pointed to a big briar patch full of blackberry bushes and brambles.

"I might push you into the river," said Brer Fox.

"Do that if you must," said Brer Rabbit, "but please, don't throw me in the briar patch."

"Or I might put you in a cage," said Brer Fox.

"Yes, do that if you like," said Brer Rabbit, "but please don't throw me in the briar patch."

Well, of course Brer Fox wanted to do the one thing Brer

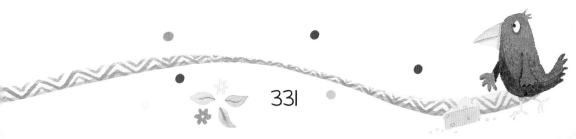

Rabbit would hate the most. So Brer Fox picked up Brer Rabbit, pulled the Tar Baby off him, whirled him round his head and threw him into the briar patch!

Smiling and feeling very pleased with himself, Brer Fox turned to set off for home. But suddenly he heard Brer Rabbit singing to himself.

Peering into the briar patch, Brer Fox saw Brer Rabbit happily cleaning off the tar from his hands and feet, and singing, "Born and bred in a briar patch! I was born and bred in a briar patch, Brer Fox!"

Brer Fox could do nothing but walk crossly home, knowing he had been tricked yet again.

The Tiger, the Hare, and the Jackal

Once upon a time, a tiger was caught in a trap. He tried to get out through the bars, but they were too narrow. As he was pushing at them and the door, a hare came by.

"Let me out of this cage!" said the tiger.

"No, my friend," replied the hare, "you would probably eat me if I did."

"Not at all!" said the tiger. "I would be your friend for ever!"

The tiger sobbed and sighed and cried and begged, so in the end the hare opened the door of the cage.

Out popped the tiger, and he

grabbed the poor hare, saying, "What a fool you are. After being in that cage for so long I am terribly hungry!"

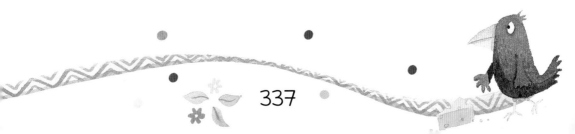

"Oh please don't eat me!" said the hare. "You promised! Besides I rescued you. You can't eat someone who rescues you!"

"Yes, I can," said the tiger. "Now get ready to be eaten."

Just then a jackal came along. He called out, "What's the matter, Mr Hare? You look as miserable as a fish out of water!"

The poor hare told the jackal what had happened.

Now the jackal was really very clever. But when it suited him he pretended to be stupid, and he did that now. "I don't understand!" he said. "Would you mind telling me again? Everything is a bit mixed up in my head."

The tiger told the story again. But the jackal shook his head, as though he still could not understand. "It's very odd," he

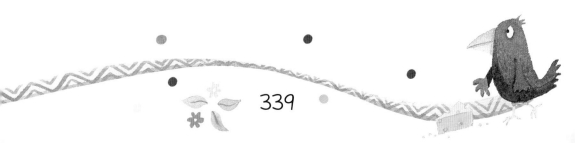

said, sadly, "but it all seems to go in one ear and come out of the other!"

"It's quite simple," said the tiger. "Why can't you understand?"

"Oh, my poor head!" cried the jackal, wringing his paws. "Let me see!

How did it begin? The hare was in the cage, and then the tiger came walking by—"

"No!" interrupted the tiger. "What a fool you are! If you can't understand better than that, I'll have to eat you too. It was me – I was in the cage!"

"Of course!" cried the jackal, pretending to tremble with fright. "Yes! I was in the cage – no, I wasn't. Dear, dear! What was it? Let me see. The tiger was in the hare, and the cage came walking by? No, that's not it, either. Well, don't mind me, but begin your dinner, for I shall never understand!"

"Yes, you shall understand!" returned the tiger, who was now very cross at how stupid the jackal was. "I'll make you understand! Look here. I am the tiger—"

"Yes!" said the jackal.

"And that is the hare—"

"Yes!"

"And that is the cage—"

"Yes!"

"And I was in the cage. Do you understand?" said the tiger.

"Yes! No. Please—"

"Well?" cried the tiger impatiently.

"Please, how did you get in?"

"How? In the usual way, of

course," said the tiger.

"Oh, dear! My head is beginning to whirl!" said the jackal. "Please don't be angry, but what is the usual way?"

At this the tiger lost patience. Jumping into the cage, he cried, "This way! This is how I got into the cage. Now do you understand?"

The jackal quickly slammed the door shut and locked it.

"Perfectly!" he cried, grinning with delight at his clever trick. "And I think you can just stay right there.

"Now, Mr Hare," the jackal continued, "let's leave this tiger in his cage and go for a walk. We must tell everyone in the jungle not to let him out again."

And with that, the hare and the jackal walked off. The tiger was back where he began,

furious at having been tricked. All he could do was roar angrily after them.

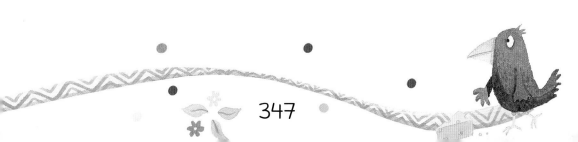

Penelope, the Wife who Waited

Penelope was married to King Odysseus, and they loved each other very much. They lived a very happy life in their beautiful palace. It was built on top of a hill looking over the

blue sea. Their bed had one leg
made from a living olive tree.
Their dining room was open to
the skies so they
could look at
the stars

while they ate. They loved to walk together in the orchards and gardens around the palace.

But one day King Odysseus had to go away to war. "Wait for me," he told Penelope. "Wait for me, and I will come back to you." Penelope promised to wait for him to return, no matter how long it took.

And so she waited and she waited. Five years went by, then

ten years. No one knew if Odysseus was still alive. Other people came back from the war, but Odysseus did not return.

Penelope believed he would still come home, but other people weren't so sure. Lords started coming to visit Penelope. "Our country needs a king," they said. "Odysseus is gone. Marry one of us. You can pick who you like, and then we will rule together."

"No! I promised Odysseus," said Penelope. "I love only him and I know he'll come home."

After a few more years, the men said, "Either marry one of us now, or we'll take over your palace and throw you out."

Poor Penelope. What could she do? Luckily, she was a very clever queen. "All right," she said. "I will pick one of you to marry.

But first I have to finish my weaving. I can't leave it half finished. If I get married I won't have time for it. Let me finish it. Then I'll marry one of you."
The men agreed.

So every day Penelope sat weaving a piece of cloth. And every night when no one could see, she pulled out all the work she'd done and started all over again.

"Haven't you finished yet?" the men asked her, and she always said, "No, not quite. Just a little more time. Please be patient. You wouldn't like to marry someone who leaves a job half done, would you?"

After twenty years had passed, Odysseus finally came

home. He was tired and much older. He arrived at the house dressed as a poor shepherd. He looked so changed that Penelope wasn't sure this really was her one true love. Other people had pretended to be Odysseus before to try to become king in his place. So she thought of a way to test him.

"Welcome," she said. "I'll tell the servants to carry our bed into the courtyard and you can rest in the sun."

But Odysseus saw through the trick. "How can you do that?" he asked. "Our bed has a leg carved from a living tree – you can't move it."

"Odysseus!" said Penelope,

laughing with happiness. "It really is you! I've waited so long."

Odysseus rid his land of all the other people who wanted to marry Penelope. And thanks to her clever trick, they lived happily ever after - and for a very long time.

Atalanta the Runner

Princess Atalanta lived long ago in ancient Greece, during a time when people believed there were many different gods and goddesses. Atalanta didn't live the usual life of a princess.

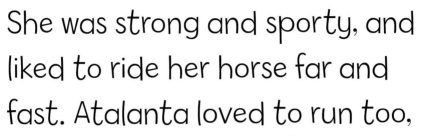

She was strong and sporty, and liked to ride her horse far and fast. Atalanta loved to run too,

and shoot with a bow and arrow. She could fish and hunt – she

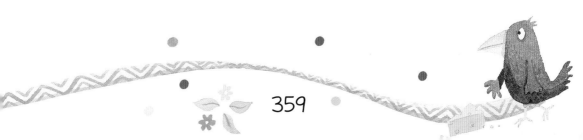

could even catch wild boar.

Many men fell in love with her because she was strong and brave. But Atalanta didn't want to get married. She wanted to live just as she was.

One day though, her father and mother said to her, "Atalanta, you are a princess and it is time you got married. You can't leave it any longer. Is there anyone at all you would like to marry?"

"No one," said Atalanta.

"You must pick someone," they said.

"Well, then," Atalanta replied. "I only want to marry someone who loves doing all the things I like. So I'll marry anyone who can beat me in a race."

It was clever of her to say that, because she knew she was faster than anyone she had ever raced before.

The king sent out the word that anyone who could beat Atalanta in a race could marry her. Many young lords and princes came to race against her, so the king built a fine, long racetrack.

Every time a man arrived who wanted to marry Atalanta, all the local people came to watch them race. And every time,

Atalanta ran ahead the whole way, while the poor man struggled after her and failed to catch up. Atalanta always won. In fact, she was hardly out of breath at all.

One man loved Atalanta above all others, and very much wanted to marry her. His name was Hippomenes, and he was a fast runner himself. But he had watched Atalanta run and he knew he couldn't beat her, no matter how hard he practised.

So, Hippomenes went to see the Greek goddess of love and begged her to help him win Atalanta's hand in marriage. She gave Hippomenes three beautiful golden apples.

"Throw these down during the race," the goddess said. "And see what happens."

Hippomenes took the apples, put them in a bag and went to run his race. Atalanta smiled as he came to the starting line. She liked this man, and almost felt she wouldn't mind marrying him – but she still wanted to win the race anyway.

"Go!" shouted the starter, and the two runners started to run. Atalanta moved easily ahead. She glanced back. Hippomenes was running well too.

Just then, Hippomenes reached into his bag and threw one of the golden apples in front of Atalanta. It flashed in the sunshine, and looked just like a real apple, only it was

much more beautiful.

Atalanta stopped running, and bent to pick up the apple, looking at it curiously. How heavy and how wonderfully made! Atalanta thought it was one of the loveliest things she had ever seen.

Suddenly, she remembered the race. Hippomenes had nearly caught up with her. Tucking the apple inside her tunic, she ran on.

Hippomenes was close behind Atalanta now, and he rolled the second apple. Atalanta couldn't leave the wonderful apple lying on the ground. Quickly, she bent down and snatched it up. She hardly took any time, but it helped Hippomenes get even closer to her.

Atalanta tucked the second apple into her tunic alongside

the first. She could hear Hippomenes coming up behind her now.

Hipppomenes now rolled the third and final apple. This time he rolled it a little to one side. Atalanta had to turn away from the track to reach for it, even though she knew she shouldn't.

As Atalanta bent down to pick up the apple, Hippomenes overtook her. She ran after him as fast as she could, but he was close to the finishing line and she couldn't catch him.

Panting hard, he crossed the line just ahead of Atalanta. He had won the race!

Hippomenes stood there, breathing hard and looking shyly at Atalanta. She looked at him and smiled. He had beaten her with a trick, but she loved the golden apples and she liked Hippomenes too. Maybe, she thought, being married wouldn't be so bad after all.

The Emperor's New Clothes

Many years ago, there lived an emperor. He was so fond of new clothes that he spent all his money on them.

One day two strangers arrived in town. They said they could

make the most beautiful material in the world. The clothes they made from the material were magic. They could only be seen by people who were clever and wise. If someone was stupid, then the clothes would be invisible to them.

"I must have a suit made from this wonderful material," said the emperor. And he gave the men money to make his suit.

The men called for the finest silks and best gold thread - but they didn't make anything with it! They packed it into their bags, planning to sell it later.

Then the men stayed in their room and pretended to work.

After a while, the emperor began to wonder how they were getting on. So he sent his Prime Minister to check.

The Prime Minister asked the two men to show him their work and the men held up nothing at all. They asked him how he liked the suit of clothes.

'Oh dear!' thought the Prime Minister, 'I can't see anything. Does that mean I am stupid? I must certainly not say that I can't see the cloth!'

So he said, "Oh, it's lovely! What colours! Yes, I will tell the emperor that it pleases me."

The cheats asked for more money, more silk, and more gold to use in their weaving. They put it all into their own pockets.

Everybody in the town was talking about the magnificent cloth. Finally the emperor himself asked to see the clothes. The cheats held out their empty hands and said they were holding the coat and the trousers. They pretended to point out the fine details – the lovely buttons,

the delicate lace, the gold-embroidered silk cloak.

'Oh no!' thought the emperor, 'I can't see anything! This is awful. Am I stupid? This is the most dreadful thing that could happen to me.'

But he didn't admit that he couldn't see the clothes, because all the people in his court were smiling and praising them.

(They couldn't see the clothes either. But they thought everyone else could, and no one wanted to look stupid.)

"Oh, they are wonderful," said the emperor. "I will wear them in the grand procession tomorrow."

The next day, the emperor took off all his clothes. The cheats pretended to put the new clothes on him.

"How beautifully they fit!" said

all the king's advisors. "What material! What colours!"

The emperor walked along in the procession, and all the people lining the streets said, "Look at the emperor's lovely new clothes!" No one wanted to admit they couldn't see them.

"But he has nothing on!" said a little boy at last. His father thought about it, and agreed. He whispered to his neighbour.

The neighbour told his friend, and soon the news spread and all the people started to laugh.

"The emperor has nothing on!" the people called out. And finally the foolish emperor realized he had been tricked. But the two cheats had long ago sneaked out of town.

Acknowledgements

Advocate Art

Kate Daubney Chicken Licken, The Enormous Turnip, The Stars in the Sky, Cat and Copy-cat, The Emperor's New Clothes **Monika Filipina** Little Red Riding Hood, The Hare and the Tortoise **Sarah Lawrence** The Gingerbread Man **Andy Rowland** The Town Mouse and the Country Mouse **Barbara Vagnozzi** Cover **Lizzie Walkley** The Crow, The Fish and the Hare, The Three Wishes, Where are the Kittens?, Brer Rabbit and the Tar Baby

The Bright Agency

Rosie Butcher Sleeping Beauty **Sharon Harmer** The Three Little Pigs **Gavin Scott** The Lion and the Mouse

Pickled Ink

Marie Simpson All decorative frames, The Magic Porridge Pot, Tikki Tikki Tembo, When the Animals got Scared, The Fox and the Crow

Plum Pudding Illustration

Francesca Assirelli Goldilocks and the Three Bears **Erica Jane Waters** The Wolf and the Seven Little Kids, King Midas has Ass's Ears, The Stupid Crocodiles, The Lion and the Two Cunning Little Jackals, Atalanta the Runner

Alessandra Psacharopulo Rumpelstiltskin, The Stone-cutter's Wishes, Icarus, the Flying Boy, The Little Red Hen and the Wheat, The Tiger, the Hare, and the Jackal

Victoria Taylor The Elves and the Shoemaker, The Three Men and the Dream, Why the Dog and Cat are Enemies, Why the Bear is Stumpy-tailed, Penelope, the Wife who Waited

Marie Simpson's illustrations © Marie Simpson 2016
All other illustrations © Miles Kelly Publishing 2016

The publisher would like to thank foxie/Shutterstock.com
for supplying the image on the endpapers

384